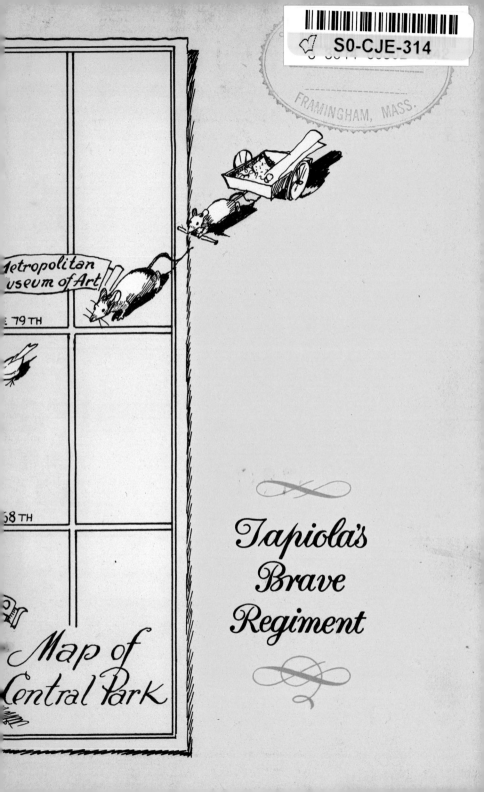

Metropolitan
useum of Art

79 TH

68 TH

Map of
Central Park

*Tapiola's
Brave
Regiment*

Robert Nathan

was born in New York City in 1894. He was educated at schools in New York and abroad, at Phillips Exeter Academy and Harvard University, where he was an editor of *The Harvard Monthly,* in which his first stories and poems appeared.

While working in an advertising agency in 1919, Mr. Nathan published his first novel, *Peter Kindred,* which has been followed by twenty volumes of poetry and prose. From his novels Mr. Nathan has acquired a reputation as a master of satiric fantasy unique in American literature, and his first editions are prized as collectors' items. His recent poetry has been widely recognized for its fine lyrical quality.

His home is in New York City, but he spends his summers on Cape Cod, where he owns a house that was built in 1810.

Tapiola's Brave Regiment

TAPIOLA'S
Brave Regiment

by ROBERT NATHAN

ILLUSTRATED BY KURT WIESE

ALFRED · A · KNOPF · NEW YORK · 1941

To Blanche and Alfred and Tapiola

Tapiola's Brave Regiment

~~~~~~~~~~~~~~~~~~~~

Tapiola's Brave Regiment

TAPIOLA was worried. Life did not seem the same to him any more. The sun shone, but its light no longer made everything look fresh and bright. The little Yorkshire terrier realized that he was getting old, and that nothing was as it used to be.

He was no larger than a small spring
chicken; and his silver colored hair hung
down almost to the floor. The little ribbon
which Mrs. Poppel fixed on his head each
day, gave him a ribald appearance, but the
fact is that he was a sensible little dog, and
had been married several times.

He did not mind growing old himself, if
only the world stayed young around him.
But it seemed to him that the world was
growing old faster than he was. When he
was young, he had wanted to be a hero; now
he was content to lead a quiet life, but the
dismal looks he saw all around him, filled
him with discouragement. "It is not at all
like the world I used to know," he said to his
friend Richard the canary, "for no one is
happy any more."

Richard, who lived in a gilded cage in the apartment below, agreed with Tapiola that things were not very encouraging. "The singers I have heard recently," he declared, "make me despair for the future. They do not care for music; their only purpose is to make the loudest possible noise. It is the fault of the critics, who do not listen, and make up reviews out of their heads." "It is a cynical generation," agreed Tapiola. "We have analyzed beauty out of existence." "What we need," said Richard gloomily, "is a return to the melodies of Schubert and Mendelssohn." "What we need," said Tapiola, "is a return to the things of the heart."

But he did not know how this was to be done.

Tapiola had many friends in the Park,

where he used to walk in the afternoon with Mrs. Poppel's maid, Margot. He often asked these friends what was wrong with the world, but each one had a different answer. "There is not enough authority," said a little white poodle, who had been taught to jump through a hoop, stand on his hind legs, and give three short barks when he was asked a question. "What we need is to be told what to do. As it is, everyone does as he likes, and the result is confusion." "Do you believe," asked Tapiola, "that we must all learn to jump through hoops?" "The important thing," said the poodle, "is to learn to obey; what you jump through does not matter."

On the other hand, Otto, the fat squirrel, complained that he could not find enough nuts any more to tide him over from one season to the next. "They are carted away from under my nose," he declared. "Perhaps the Park is more tidy that way, but what happens to the individual and his savings?" "May I ask," exclaimed a starling, "why you should have savings? I have none; and neither has any of my friends. Let us all share what there is; no person should have more than another." "I work very hard for what I get," said Otto; and he added proudly: "I believe in laying aside something for the future." "The future," cried the starling scornfully; "one belly does not make a future. What chance have the starlings to put anything by?" "I have not noticed them doing any work," said Otto. "Somebody has to think the great thoughts," replied the starling.

Shortly after this, Tapiola awoke one night with a beating heart. He realized that he would have to die some day, and that he was afraid of death. The next morning, he went to pay a call on his friend Henry, a pigeon who lived with his wife Matilda under one of the cornices of the north buttress of Saint Patrick's Cathedral. "I cannot bear to die," he said to the pigeon, "because I do not know what it is like."

"I am sorry for you," said Henry. "To face death without religion, is a horrible experience." These words caused Tapiola to feel more miserable than ever. "But what," he asked, "if you do not believe in heaven, and the other comforts?" "One can believe anything," replied Henry, "if one has to."

He continued: "What the world needs today is faith, for only faith can cope with the evils of these times."

And he gazed about, in search of his wife, but he could not find her. "What was I saying?" he asked unhappily.

"You were speaking of the evil of these times," said Tapiola.

"So I was," said Henry; "so I was. I think I can honestly say that I deprecate it."

"We must all die," said Tapiola, "and one would think that anything so inevitable would not keep us awake at night. Yet Mr. Poppel, the great publisher, seems just as worried as I am."

Henry stood beneath the north buttress of the Cathedral, from where it was possible to see the tall gray spires rising into the sky among the shops and office buildings. It was a landscape of indescribable grandeur, but he did not seem to notice it. Presently there was a muffled squawk, and Matilda shot out from around a corner, with a dazzled air. She was not alone; and her expression was tender and dreamy. Seeing her husband, she stopped in confusion, and retreated behind the corner again. "Ah," said Henry happily. "Now I know where she is."

And he added, with a thoughtful look, "We all have our worries, unfortunately."

Tapiola returned home; and that evening, in the apartment downstairs, he said to Richard the canary,

"Who will give us faith again in the world?"

That night, as he lay in his wicker basket with its silk pillow and its eiderdown quilt,

his heart was filled with uncertainty. He
longed for a divine friend, with a tail that
swept the skies, who would say to him in a
voice full of sweetness, "Do not be afraid,
Tapiola, for I love you, and will not let anything happen to you."

After a while he fell asleep. Then he
dreamed of a world in which the tiger roamed
at will, and great herds of giant aurochs
swept across the wastes which had once been
his home. Finally a large black dog took hold
of him by the leg, and declared, "I do not
like you."

Tapiola whined and twitched in his basket,
under the eiderdown quilt. In the morning
he said to himself, "I believe that this dream
is a warning, and that some disaster is about
to overtake the world." But Richard believed

that Tapiola had eaten too much supper the night before. "I did not dream about anything," said Richard, "and this morning I feel very well." "Just the same, I believe it is a warning," said Tapiola.

Otto, the gray squirrel, agreed with him. "For some time past," he said, "I have thought of moving to the west, possibly as far as New Jersey; some instinct tells me that I should be safer on the other side of the Orange Mountains." "Then you also believe," said Tapiola, "that some danger threatens us?" "I do not know what to believe," said Otto, "but I mean to save myself, if possible." "If there is danger," said Tapiola slowly, "I do not think that we ought to run away from it."

And Henry, when Tapiola next saw him,

expressed the opinion that if disaster were near, the faithful should prepare to meet it with a joyful heart, and with a quiet mind. "I have heard of a comet," he declared, "and there are other portents. Perhaps the end of the world is coming; in that case, the trump of doom will be heard even in New Jersey, and your friend will be fried to a crisp just as rapidly in Summit or Short Hills as he would be in Central Park." "I do not believe it is the end of the world," said Tapiola, "but I believe it is something."

So saying, he went home, and hid under the sofa, to think things out.

In this favorite retreat, silent, dusty, and dark, Tapiola felt safe from the ordinary surprises of life. Now, with the strong roof of the sofa above him, he wondered if it

might not be a good idea to give up, and
simply stay where he was. But then he remembered how on cleaning days the sofa was
moved from one end of the room to the other,
and he exclaimed,

"It is only in ourselves that safety lies, since the strongest shelter can be attacked from the rear."

And he said to himself: "Whatever is cooking in the world, I must try to face it in a resolute manner."

In this mood he approached Richard again, and asked for his opinion. After considering the matter for a while with his head on one side, the canary replied that he did not think that anything was cooking among the musicians. "I am willing to believe," he said, "that your friend Otto prefers to live in New Jersey; but I do not see what that has to do with me."

To this Tapiola replied earnestly: "We are in danger, Richard; there is a menace in the air, which I can feel, even if I cannot

describe it. Henry believes that the end of
the world is at hand. In any event, the future
rises before us dark as a wave at night. Are
we to sit by, and let it sweep over us? I believe that we should struggle against it with
all our strength. Then, if we die, we shall
drown like heroes, rather than be beached
like herring." "If the end of the world is at
hand," said Richard, "we are already
beached."

Nevertheless, he was willing to listen to
what Tapiola had to say, for he was tired of
sitting day after day in his cage, with nothing to do. "I intend," said Tapiola, "to
gather together a small company of heroes,
who will defend each other from whatever is
coming, and who will stand together in any
event." "That is an interesting idea," said

Richard, "and you are the one to do it. But I must think of my career." "If the aurochs come," said Tapiola, "you will not have a career." "I do not know any aurochs," said Richard, "but I will think it over, and I will let you know." "We shall need music," said Tapiola, "to keep up the spirits of the regiment." "Ah," said Richard, "so we are already a regiment. That is good; by all means let us take a few others with us, for safety's sake."

The next day Tapiola went to see Henry at the Cathedral. "I am raising a regiment," he told him, "to defend ourselves against the aurochs; and I should like to have you join me." Henry received this invitation with surprise, and gazed for some time at the sky before replying. "I should have to leave Matilda," he said at last in trembling tones. "I do not believe that it could be arranged." "She would forgive you," said Tapiola. "Perhaps she would," said Henry, "but I do not like to think so.

"Besides," he added a moment later, "what is an aurochs?" "It is a sort of bull, with horns," said Tapiola. "Does it fly?" asked Henry. "I do not think so," said Tapiola, "but it lays everything waste." "It is probably a grasshopper," said Henry.

But presently he grew gloomy again and shook his head. "What am I thinking of?" he cried. "After all, I am connected with a cornice of the north buttress of the Cathedral. I cannot simply give up my position, and go off, like that." "You have said," remarked Tapiola, "that faith alone can give us courage. We, who prepare to face death, will need the comforts of religion." "I had not thought of that," said Henry.

And he agreed to join the regiment, in a spiritual capacity.

That night Tapiola heard, rising from the open window of the apartment below, the most lugubrious sounds; and the next day Richard admitted that he had been practising "taps," and also the Soldier's Lament. "Would it not be better to attempt something a little gayer," asked Tapiola, "such as The Campbells Are Coming, or Bonnie Prince Charlie?" "I am willing to try," said Richard, "but I believe that I excel in the more serious forms." "While you are practising," said Tapiola, "I will see about getting started."

And he returned upstairs, with a martial
air, and in a mood of excitement. Noticing
how he was parading about, wagging his
tail, and uttering short barks, Mrs. Poppel
immediately sent him out onto the street
with Margot, the maid, to do his duty. He
returned, sobered by this experience, and retired once more beneath the sofa, to think
things over.

Tapiola knew that he was not a very good
organizer, and that he needed someone to
help him. "For courage is not enough," he
thought, "even when accompanied by music.
I should like to find someone with practical
experience, to tell me how to start out; after
that, it ought to be a simple matter to keep
going."

But he could not think of anyone to ask;

and he never would have got started at all if he had not had the good fortune to run across a travelling companion of other days, in the person of an aged rat who had been called in by Otto to help him move his possessions to the west. "We will deliver them in New Jersey in good order," the rat was saying, as Tapiola went by, "but I must tell you that we cannot be responsible for the effects of dampness, rot, sprouting, maggots, riots, or catastrophes of nature." "That does not leave you very much to be responsible for," said Otto doubtfully. "How do I know that you are to be trusted?" "A good name is rather to be chosen than great riches," said the rat, "and loving favor than silver and gold."

At these words, Tapiola recognized Jeremiah, and joyously embracing his old friend, exclaimed, "It is a long time since I have seen you, Jeremiah. What have you been doing; and how is it that I find you engaged in the moving business?" "I have been engaged in many businesses," replied Jeremiah, "some fat, some lean. One must make money where money is to be made; and if people wish to move, somebody must move them." "Jeremiah," cried Tapiola, who knew his friend, "confess that you do not have even so much as a wheelbarrow to move them in." "Well," said Jeremiah, looking nervously around, "I am negotiating for something." "You are incorrigible," said Tapiola.

"Tell me about yourself," said Jeremiah, "and the little rabbit that you brought home with you from the journey." "She has left me," said Tapiola gravely. "I am sorry to hear it," said Jeremiah. "And how is Richard, that distinguished baritone?" "He is a tenor now," said Tapiola, "but it has not helped him any." "What he needs is an agent," said Jeremiah. "I must have a talk with him." "As a matter of fact," said Tapiola, "he is giving up his career for the time being, in order to join my regiment." "What," cried Jeremiah in surprise, "have you a regiment? But I am not astonished, for I remember very well how you vanquished the beetle." "I do not have a regiment yet," said Tapiola, "but I mean to have one, as soon as I can find out how it is done." "Then you have come to the right place," declared Jeremiah, "for I know all about it."

And gazing down his nose, he assumed a

thoughtful air. "In the first place," he said,
"it is necessary to have supplies of all kinds."
"I had not thought of that," said Tapiola.
"It will be difficult to procure them," said
Jeremiah; "I do not believe that there are
any to be had." "Then there is nothing left
but the sofa," said Tapiola unhappily. "Do
not be in such a hurry," said Jeremiah. "I
did not say positively."

He continued: "I am not optimistic; but
it is possible that I might still be able to procure a few of the most necessary articles,
though I believe that I should be more successful if I had an official position in the
company." "You can be Quartermaster,"
said Tapiola eagerly, "in charge of supplies." "You would not care to make it Quartermaster General?" asked Jeremiah. "I do

not care at all," said Tapiola. "I have always wanted to be a General," said Jeremiah.

"But who," he asked presently, "are the enemy?" "I do not know," said Tapiola. "I only know that they are fierce and bold. I saw them in a dream; they came from the dark ages of the past, to lay waste the earth. Their hair was shaggy, and long, and their hooves thundered on the plains. They were the aurochs; or so they described themselves." "The aurochs are extinct," said Jeremiah. "They have popped up again," said Tapiola.

It was agreed that Jeremiah was to furnish the regiment with supplies, on a commission basis; and that there would be a general meeting soon at which the regiment would be mustered in. Tapiola then saluted

Jeremiah, and went home, to look over his possessions, in order to decide what to take with him to the wars. He did not think that he would need his ball, or his bone made of rubber; and he feared that his wicker basket with its pillow might be out of place. However, he decided to carry with him his eider-down quilt, in case there should not be blankets enough; and also several small squares of paper, in case he were kept indoors by bad weather.

Richard, meanwhile, had decided upon a piece of dried apple, and a little package of seeds. But he assured Tapiola that he was not only thinking of himself. "We are old friends, you and I," he said. "I need not tell you that what is mine, is yours. I see that you are taking along a warm quilt for the cold

~~~~~~~~~~~~~~~~~~~~~~~~~~~~~~~

winter nights." "You may come under it if you like," said Tapiola, "for I feel that I am responsible for your health. Whom would you like notified, in case of death?" "What do you mean, death?" exclaimed Richard; "what a way to talk." "We are going to war," said Tapiola; "we shall be in the front rank of battle." "Do not dispose of me so recklessly," said Richard. "I shall be in the rear, with the music."

Shortly after this, Tapiola started to work on a farewell address to his mistress Mrs. Poppel. "Farewell," he said, "friend of my youth, you who have been my teacher and my guide. It was you who taught me to play with my ball, to use the little squares of newspaper every day, and to stay quietly in my basket in the morning. If this was not

in itself a great career, it is nevertheless true
that nobody asked anything more of me, except myself. I am glad that you were not dis-
appointed in me, and that you did not wish
me to be a mastiff, or a great Dane, like Ch.
Lance von Habich. That was my own concern; you were content to love me for myself
alone. Here, within these walls, I have spent
my happiest years; here, beneath this sofa, I
have enjoyed long hours without a care.
Now those careless hours are over; and the
peaceful days are ended. Farewell, dear
home, and also my basket, in which I have
been so comfortable. My country calls me,
and I must go; only the mighty can be indifferent to tyranny, the small must fight or
perish. Friend and benefactress, more than
a mother, farewell; think kindly of me, and

~~~~~~~~~~~~~~~~~~~~~~~~~~~~~

forgive me for any sorrow that I may have caused you."

This recital, or rather rehearsal, for there was no one else present, moved Tapiola greatly, and there were tears in his eyes when he ended. He wished to find somebody who would take care of Mrs. Poppel when he was gone; and seeing a small household bug disappearing under the sofa, he stopped him, and said, "I should like to entrust Mrs. Poppel to you, for I am leaving soon at the head of my regiment." "I do not know Mrs. Poppel," said the bug; and went off and hid in a crack in the wall.

A week now went by, during which nothing further was heard from Jeremiah, a fact which caused Richard to become very impatient, and to remark, "We have missed the boat." At the end of this time Tapiola received a message that all was in readiness, and that the regiment would be mustered on the following day. That night Tapiola went to bed early, and for the last time, in his wicker basket with the silk pillow; but he was unable to sleep. And as the hours of darkness went by, he prayed that he would be a good soldier, and not run away when it was time to meet the foe.

E A R L Y next morning a
small procession might have been seen emerging from the apartment house where Mrs.
Poppel lived. Richard came first, singing
with all his might; the tune he had chosen
was The Stars And Stripes Forever. Behind
him, with a proud expression, marched Tapi-

ola; a red ribbon in his hair added to his martial appearance, and the eiderdown blanket
was slung across his back at a rakish angle,
like a Hussar's jacket. Henry followed,
looking very solemn; and behind him, bring-
ing up the rear, was Jeremiah, with the supplies. These consisted of a piece of yellow
cheese, a roll of lint for bandages, half a
dozen assorted buttons, a map of Europe for
the year 1840, and a large nail, or spike,
"such," said Jeremiah, "as Jael used upon
the head of Sisera." These supplies were
piled in a small wagon, drawn by Jeremiah's
grandson, Micah, whom Jeremiah had
drafted into service.

Their appearance was greeted by a cheer
from several friends and acquaintances who
had come to see them off. Among these was

Otto, who wished to find out why his furniture had not been moved to New Jersey. Stirred by the music, however, and by the noble appearance of the regiment, he forgot about his furniture, and rushing up to Tapiola, presented him with a small bag of peanuts, which he had been saving for a rainy day. "Brave Tapiola," he exclaimed, "I am only sorry that my business affairs do not allow me to join you." "This is a generous

gift," said Tapiola, "and I accept it for freedom's sake."

The starling, on the other hand, loudly de-
plored these martial preparations. "Haven't
we trouble enough at home," he asked bit-
terly, "without going out to look for it, besides? Let us feed our own birds, before we
start saving the world." "God will feed His
birds," said Henry sternly. "Then let Him
feed His squirrels also," said the starling.
"You are a communist," said Henry.

At these words, Matilda ran forward and
embraced him. "How splendid you look," she
exclaimed, "and with such a fiery air. I have
made you a little feather boa, to keep you
from getting a sore throat. If in the past I
have ever been remiss in my wifely duties,
forgive me." "Farewell, Matilda," said

Henry in trembling tones. "Whatever you may have done to me in the past, I forgive you." "I will pray for you every day," said Matilda, turning away to hide her emotion.

But as she passed the starling, she stumbled, and uttered a cry. "I am a widow," she said faintly; "ah me." "You are very young to be a widow," said the starling, gazing at her in admiration. "May I take you home?" "Please do," murmured Matilda. "I will show you the Cathedral."

Bathed in the clear light of morning, the regiment proceeded toward its rendezvous in the Park. Tapiola breathed in the fresh air, with its sweet odors of spring, and filled with a respect for nature and for his own historic mission, he remarked,

"Life is a struggle, in which the strongest

~~~~~~~~~~~~~~~~~~~~~~~~~~~~~~~~~~~~~

survives. The trees of the forest, the flowers of the field, vie with each other for the sun. All nature is in balance; life and death, good and evil, tremble upon the scales." "You have read that somewhere," said Richard; "it has an artful sound." "Do not be afraid of art," said Tapiola, "for it only tells us what we know, in a nobler form."

They continued marching; and presently Richard burst forth: "Of all arts, music is the most profound. For it inspires the soul, without having to make any conversation about it. Yet, of all critics of the arts, those of music are the most talkative. If anything is artful, they know it; but if it is noble, they do not understand it." "In literature it is just the opposite," said Tapiola.

Behind them, in the rear, Micah turned

to his grandfather. "This is the sort of war I enjoy," he remarked, "where the work is not too heavy, and everything is very interesting. However, I should like to know when we are to meet the enemy, for I am anxious to win promotion." "Do not be impatient," said Jeremiah; "you will be promoted in due course, and when the time comes. In the meanwhile, try to improve yourself, since your future is not very encouraging, in any case."

Drawn up on the parade ground behind the Museum, Tapiola surveyed his command. With a flashing eye, and in a ringing voice, he exclaimed: "Officers and men of the Twenty Seventh, I am proud to take command of this regiment, whose motto is 'Success,' and whose intention is never to re-

treat." He then asked Henry to invoke a
blessing. The regiment stood with bent
heads, while Henry prayed: "Lord, we who
are among the smallest of Your creatures,
entreat You: look down upon us, and shelter us with Your wings. Help us to see what
is right, and give us the courage to defend
it. We are not proud or mighty in Your
sight, but humble; for it is said that not even

a sparrow may fall, without You. Bless us in our dealings with one another; guard us against the foe; strengthen our faith in heaven; and remember in loving-kindness those we leave behind."

After this, Jeremiah presented Tapiola with a silk banner in the colors of the regiment, and with the motto "Success to Harry's Delicatessen"; and Richard burst out with an aria from Rossini's "William Tell."

The regiment then bivouacked for the night, and Tapiola called a council of officers, to consider the situation.

"Gentlemen," he said, when they were gathered around him, "we do not know where the enemy is, so we do not know whether we are in danger or not. On the other hand, the wise commander does not wait until he is attacked, to take precautions." And he arranged for Richard to keep a sharp watch from a tree. "You, Henry," he added, "are to be in reserve; while Jeremiah keeps open our line of supply." "I shall be dizzy all alone in a tree," said Richard. "What if I fall out?" "In that case," said Tapiola, "let Henry keep watch, while you stay on the ground, in support." "I do not object to keeping open the line of supply," said Jeremiah, "but I must remind you that you already owe me for a pound of cheese, a large nail, and a map. I will not charge you for the buttons, because they did not cost me anything."

Undoing the little collar around his neck, Tapiola handed it to Jeremiah in silence.

"The plate is of silver," he said, "and the leather is good. Let me hear no more about what I owe you." "The buckle is of brass," said Jeremiah, putting it in his mouth, "but I am not complaining."

Left by himself to guard the supply wagon, Micah sat down and looked around. He had never been in the Park before, never so far away from home; the sky above the Museum was very blue, and wider than he had imagined. He looked at the green lawns, and at the budding trees; he saw the obelisk on its hill, and he believed that he was in the wilderness, a stone's thrown from Egypt. He felt a little frightened, but he meant to be a good soldier, and since no one was looking, he ate a little cheese to keep his spirits up.

He knew that he was young and ignorant, and that he had a great deal to learn. Life was an endless path in front of him, there were many golden years ahead, with opportunities for improvement. He did not feel in the least discouraged about the future; his heart beat, and he said to himself, "Perhaps some day I too shall be a success, like my grandfather Jeremiah."

These reflections, and others like them, were interrupted by a little female mouse, who came out from under a bench, and said to him in a friendly voice, "What are you thinking about, sitting there so solemn, and all?"

Micah was startled; but he was innocent and truthful, and he replied: "I am thinking about life and death, and how to get along in

the world; and I am eating a little cheese, to
tide me over until my supper." "You are a
stranger here, are you not?" asked the
mouse; "for I do not remember ever having
seen you before." "My regiment has just
moved in," said Micah. "Then you are a soldier," said the mouse. "How exciting."

And she added, "I hope you will not let
anybody hurt me."

Wrinkling her nose, she approached the
wagon in an artless way, and gave one or two
delicate sniffs. "That is a very fragrant
cheese," she said. "I suppose that it belongs
to the army." "Would you like a little?"
asked Micah. "I should love it," said the
mouse.

And climbing up onto the wagon, she
settled herself next to Micah with an ami-

able air. "What is your name?" she asked.
"And what do you like to do best in all the
world?" "My name is Micah," said Micah,
"and I do not know what I like to do best,
for I am young, and I have not had very
much experience." At this the mouse let out
a silvery peal of laughter. "Have you no
sweetheart?" she asked. "Do not ask me to
believe it, for you soldiers are all alike." "I
have a mother," said Micah.

"I do not see what that has to do with it,"
said the mouse.

Presently she remarked, in a thoughtful
way, "But perhaps you are ambitious, and I
have misjudged you." "I do not know about
that," said Micah simply, "but it is true that
I can hardly wait to become an officer."
"Ah," said the mouse, sighing, "it is refresh-

ing to find someone to talk to upon serious subjects."

And she daintily swallowed some cheese. "My name is Amy," she said, when she had got it down, "and I do not have many friends. Perhaps I will come and see you again some time, for I, too, am lonely." "Please do," said Micah, "for I am sure that I should enjoy it." "Good-bye now," said Amy, and getting down from the wagon, she disappeared beneath the bench.

That night Micah wrote to his mother:

"Dear Ma,

We are not organized very well yet; on account of the war is only beginning. I have met a very Nice frend. Her name is Amy, and she is a serius mous. there is nothing to

do yet in the war, we just sit around and I
have charge of the waggon where the cheese
is. It is all right in the rejiment, granpa is
well also. Maybe I should have some serius
books to read. I am lerning to become an
oficer. Amy is only a mous, but she has a
serius mind. Well, I must go now.

Yrs. Very Truly,

Micah."

At the same time, Jeremiah appeared before Tapiola in a state of the greatest excitement. "To arms," he cried. "The war has
begun." "Are you sure?" asked Tapiola anx-
iously; "I have heard no alarms." "Nevertheless, the enemy is upon us," replied Jeremiah; "half our cheese is gone." "Turn out

the guard," said Tapiola, and ordered Richard to sound the alert.

That night the regiment stood to its arms, but no enemy appeared; and in the morning the starlings on the roof of the Museum took up their noisy quarrels as before. Shortly after daybreak, a letter was handed to Jeremiah; it was from his daughter, Micah's mother.

"Dear Pa," it read, "I have been awake all night, thinking about my son. I wonder does he get enough to eat; and please do not let him get his feet wet. I should like him to have some regular exercise, and to be home by Saturday night. I am sending him a little woolen cap, and a chocolate cake, which he likes; also a little box of pills which they tell

me have a very good laxative effect. Aunt
Clara sends love. We are all very proud to
have a General in the family.

> Your affectionate daughter,
>> Sarah.

P.S. Who is Amy?"

This letter did not surprise Jeremiah, who
showed it to Henry with the remark, "A
mother's worries are never done." "What
woman," said Henry, "having ten pieces of
silver, if she lose one piece, doth not light a
lamp, and sweep the house, and seek dili-
gently until she find it?" "That is all very
well," said Jeremiah, "but what does she
mean by Amy?"

Henry did not know. "Perhaps it is a
secret code," he said. "I do not think so,"
said Jeremiah, "for I have always heard that

it takes two to make a secret." "Not in my family," said Henry, a little sadly.

As the morning wore on, Tapiola climbed the hill behind the Museum, from which it was possible to study the immediate terrain, and also the more distant horizon. There the rooftops of the city, soaring above the shadowy streets, presented a vision of crags and peaks blue and mysterious in the air. He was accompanied by Richard who, seeing for the first time this lofty panorama, exclaimed: "We are secure; no enemy can reach us. Let us go home, and forget the war." "On the contrary," said Tapiola, "those very buildings will serve as a shield to the foe."

And he began to make a diagram of the position. "How is it," asked Richard, "that you know so much about military matters?"

To which Tapiola replied, "I have studied
the campaigns of General Gamelin." "Was
he a dog," asked Richard, "or a canary?"
"He turned out to be a canary," said Tapiola.

"Go aloft, Richard," said Tapiola presently, "and tell me what you see." "I will fly
toward the lake," said Richard proudly,
"and reconnoiter." "If you sight the enemy,"
said Tapiola, "return at full speed; do not
risk an engagement with superior numbers."
"Perhaps," said Richard, swallowing, "it
would be better if Henry went with me."
"Henry is busy elsewhere," said Tapiola.
"Well," said Richard, "I will go, but I am
not as eager as I was."

Left to himself, Tapiola gazed out upon
the peaceful city, bathed in the warm rays of

the sun. Everyone, he thought, must find his own city most beautiful. For each city is a way of life, different from every other way. And we must respect a way of life even if it is not our own. Beauty has many faces; the tiger also was shaped by an immortal hand and eye, according to the poet, Mr. Blake. I should not like to live in the jungle amidst the thickets of bamboo; but that is a proper spot for Tigers, who would feel out of place under the sofa at Mrs. Poppel's.

"What is more," he added sternly, "if they wish the sofa, they will have to fight for it."

And he gave a ferocious growl.

At this an elderly sparrow, who had been watching him with some curiosity, jumped into the air with surprise. "Bless my soul," he exclaimed. "Where are the police?"

~~~~~~~~~~~~~~~~~~~~~~~~~~~~~~~

"There is no cause for alarm," said Tapiola; "control yourself." "That is all very well," said the sparrow, "but the police are never around when you want them."

And he added uneasily, "All this growling and barking."

"You are in the way here," said Tapiola, trying to look past him; "I must ask you to remove yourself from the field of fire." "Do not try to order me about," said the sparrow testily; "my name is Peabody, and I am the head of a large concern." "Just the same," said Tapiola, "I wish you would go away." "Nonsense," said the sparrow; "I shall stay where I am." "You are interfering with the war," cried Tapiola. "The war makes no difference to me," said the sparrow. "I shall do business with whoever wins."

~~~~~~~~~~~~~~~~~~~~~~~~~~~~~~

Meanwhile Richard, winging his way above the lake, and gazing down at the dark blue water ruffled by the breeze, was thinking about his mission, with regret. It is all very well for Tapiola, he thought, for he simply stays on the ground, and gives orders. And if I were an eagle, I might enjoy what I am doing. But a tenor, even a tenor robusto, is at a disadvantage, suspended in the air several hundred feet above a lake.

He remembered what Tapiola had said about superior numbers, and he shivered. Alas, he thought, why was I not content to stay in my little cage, with its yellow, sandy floor, and let others fight the war if they felt like it? Then, when it was over, there would still be somebody left in the world to sing. But no; I allowed myself to be swept away

by my emotions; with the result that I am
sent out upon a dangerous errand, all alone,
before lunch.

Richard, you are a fool; but it is too late
now.

At this moment, strains of music wafted
upward upon the air, caused him to slacken
his pace, and to head downward, in surprise,
toward a small round building half hidden
among some trees. It is the Opera House, he
thought, and there is a performance going
on.

As he drew nearer, he recognized the
strains of O Sole Mio, and, a little later, the
opening bars of the Marseillaise. Circling
about, he found a seat on a rail outside the
building, and prepared himself to listen, in
silence. But presently, since no one else

seemed to be singing, he opened his mouth, and tried a few notes. After that, he continued to sing as loudly as he could. He sang the Miserere from Trovatore, the Soldier's March from Faust, and the Anvil Chorus. "I am not getting any applause," he said to himself, "but I am having a very good time."

The music stopped; smiling, and with a satisfied expression, he rose again into the air above the Opera House over the door of which was painted in golden letters the word "Carousel."

In the best of spirits, humming to himself, he travelled eastward, not knowing that the Zoo lay in that direction.

Ten minutes later, pale and trembling, he flung himself out of the sky, at Tapiola's feet. "To arms," he cried hoarsely; "the enemy is upon us." "What," cried Tapiola, also turning pale, "do you mean that you have seen him?" "He is encamped beyond the lake," said Richard, "in great numbers." "Have you really," asked Tapiola, licking his dry lips, "seen a tiger?" "I have seen three of them," answered Richard, "and an aurochs." "What did it look like?" whispered Tapiola. "Like a camel," said Richard. "Turn out the guard," croaked Tapiola. "To arms."

They found Micah asleep in the shade under the supply wagon. "I suppose this is part of a soldier's life," he groaned, struggling to his feet, and trying to rub the sleep out of his eyes, "but I would rather meet the enemy face to face, than be turned out so often." "Be glad that you are able to serve your country," said Tapiola; and Jeremiah added: "Be happy that your sleep was not like that of Samson, who was shorn of his strength by the Philistines." "I had a most wonderful dream," said Micah. "I dreamt that I was alone in a meadow fragrant with aniseed. The flowers bloomed, and crickets hopped about among the weeds. Presently my mother approached me, with a book; it was by a young poet, and it was made of cheese. We started to eat it; my mouth was full of blissful feelings, when I noticed that it was not my mother beside me, but Amy."

"Oh ho," said Jeremiah.

"Hum," said Henry.

And they exchanged a thoughtful glance.

"Then I woke up," said Micah.

And he went and took his position in the line.

The sun passed through the zenith, the shadows of afternoon lengthened in the grass. A robin sang his liquid song, and nursemaids took their children home from play. The old blue mist of twilight gathered in the hollows; in the sky, evening shone like a lamp behind the city. High in the clear green air, a wedge of duck flew north; and in the south, a few faint roars were heard as the keepers fed the animals at the Zoo. Twittering, the starlings on the roof of the Museum, settled down to sleep. "Stand fast, the Twenty Seventh," said Tapiola.

In the soft spring dusk, Jeremiah approached his commander. "Sir," he said, "would it not be wise for you to rest? for you have been under a severe strain. Henry and I will keep watch, although I do not believe that anything will develop before daybreak." "Brave Jeremiah," exclaimed Tapiola, "and also brave Henry, you are right, I am very weary. I shall go to sleep for a little while; but I must ask you to waken me at the first sign of danger." "I will go to sleep, too," said Richard, "though it will be chilly, all by myself." "You may come under my quilt," said Tapiola.

And he made room for his friend, beside him.

THE great columns of the Milky Way marched in the dark above them; one by one the far-off lights of the city went out, leaving the Park a shadowy pool within the shadowy night. And Jeremiah, alone upon his hill near the obelisk, thought to himself, So it has always been, that some must watch the night, while others rest, to greet the day. So it was that we watched in Egypt, and in Rome, while those who slept still sleep, forever unwaking. Thus David waked, at Eng-Edi, while the King slumbered; and yet Another, at Gethsemane, saying "Could ye not watch with me one hour?" Far off, beyond the farthest star, rises tomorrow's wind and sun; and here, smaller than the smallest tree, I stand, looking and listening.

A near-by rustle took him by surprise; his heart beat, his whiskers bristled, and he exclaimed in a hoarse whisper, "Who is there?"

"Is it you, Micah?" answered a sweet voice. "This is Amy."

"Micah is asleep," said Jeremiah. "I am his grandfather."

He could hear the little mouse catch her breath. "Not," she said faintly, "the great General?" "I see that you have heard of me," said Jeremiah. "Naturally," said Amy; and she drew nearer in an innocent way, but with a wheedling motion. "That is very gratifying," said Jeremiah, "but just the same, I must ask you what you are doing within the lines so late at night?" "I have only come," said Amy humbly, "to bring Micah a little present of salami." "Hard or soft?" asked Jeremiah. "Soft," said Amy. "I will take it to him," said Jeremiah, "in the morning."

"I am so glad to meet you at last," said Amy. "I have heard so much about you." "Have you indeed?" said Jeremiah uneasily; "hm." "I had no idea that you would look so young," said Amy; "a General . . . you must be very brave." "I try to do my duty," said Jeremiah. "But of course you are modest," said Amy. "All great Generals are modest.

"I like older people," she said, moving daintily against him. "They are more sympathetic. I think that sympathy is a very fine thing, don't you?" "It is indeed," said Jeremiah heartily. "It is indeed." "One is more attractive when one has suffered," said Amy.

"Young people are so . . . so empty."
"Quite so," said Jeremiah. And he added
tenderly, "You have suffered?"

"I lead a lonely life," said Amy with a
sigh; and for a moment she allowed her head
to rest against the General's soft fur. "I am
alone," she said. "My poor," murmured
Jeremiah. "I see that you understand me,"
said Amy. "It is such a comfort to be under-
stood." "You are so young and tender," said
Jeremiah huskily; "I do not like to think
that you are lonely." "My," said Amy; "you
are a poet, too."

And she let her head sink once more upon
his shoulder.

But a moment later she drew away, with
a faint cry. "What am I doing?" she cried.
"I know that you soldiers are all alike. What

must you think of me?" "Only the best," said
Jeremiah, breathing with difficulty. "Now
you are making fun of me," said Amy with
a pout. "How can I believe you?" "Feel how
my heart is beating," said Jeremiah. "Indeed
I am not making fun of you." "It is very
light up here on top of the hill," said Amy;
"it would be cosier down below, among the
bushes."

And she slipped away, with a backward
glance, and a slight smile. A few moments
later a wren who had been asleep in a bush
below the obelisk, rose from her bed with an
exclamation of annoyance. "It is getting
very crowded here," she declared.

And Henry, in a tree above the walk to
the little pond on which, during the sunny
hours of the day, children had been sailing

their boats, gazed through the darkness in the direction of the Cathedral, and thought of Matilda. "Where are you now, Matilda," he said, "under some cornice, dreaming? It is not the first time I have been awake, watching the night for your sake; but then it used to be only yourself from whom I wished to guard you. Now it is a more terrifying, though perhaps on the whole a less implacable foe. For it is in us, ourselves, that we must look for the host and body of our deaths; and those who come to do us harm, but break a vessel which in any event must soon be broken. If we cling to this little station above the endless waters, it is because that is all we have to cling to: the yellow flower of day, the rose of evening, are all that we know of life, here or hereafter. The heart clings to that which it knows; and I to you, Matilda, even if in your dreams you smile to see another face than mine. For I believe that our knowledge is but a drop; and that He who made us, forgives us."

The dawn brightened in the east, behind the shadowy blue houses, as the sun, still seaward, turned the sky to apricot. And Tapiola, shivering, sneezed and woke, to find himself outside the quilt, and Richard beneath it. Yawning, he arose, and went to inspect the lines.

He found Jeremiah at his post; but the Quartermaster General looked strangely bedraggled. "Jeremiah," cried Tapiola in alarm, "old friend—what has happened? Are you wounded?" "It is nothing," said Jeremiah modestly. At the same time, he sat

down, as though his legs were no longer able
to support him. "There has been a battle,"
exclaimed Tapiola. "Alas! why was I not
awakened?" "There was a slight skirmish in
the bushes," Jeremiah admitted, "but I believe that I was able to take care of it myself,
and in any event I did not wish to bother you
with it." "You seem to have lost half your
whiskers," said Tapiola. "I must admit,"
said Jeremiah, "that I was warmly engaged."

Tapiola returned to his headquarters, and
composed a general order, in honor of this
victory, which he characterised as showing
audacity, boldness, courage, and initiative, as
well as demonstrating the power of defense.
And Micah, with a tremulous smile wrote
home to his mother that the family had al-

ready distinguished itself in action. "Perhaps I too," he wrote shyly, "will some day
win a battle, like Grandfather, and then they
will make me a Corporal."

During the next few hours, the nail, or
spike, was set up and prepared for action
under Richard's direction; while Tapiola retired to the shade of a tree, to study the map
of Europe for 1840, which was a part of the
supplies. "Here," he said to Jeremiah, "is
our position"; marking a spot midway between Munich and the Black Forest; "and
here, below this lake, according to Richard, is
the foe. Since he cannot cross the lake which
looks to be at least fifty miles long, and since,
according to this map, there are high mountains all along its eastern border, it stands to
reason that he will make his strongest bid in

the west, between the Mall, and the Drive."
"It would be a simple matter to bomb him,"
said Jeremiah thoughtfully, "as he comes out
of the tunnel at Seventy-Eighth street." "A
very excellent maneuver," said Tapiola.
"Tell Henry to be ready."

Richard was then ordered out on recon-
naisance, to report the first sign of enemy
movement, and the regiment settled down to
await developments. These were not forth-
coming; but during the course of the afternoon, several parties of sight-seers visited the
camp, including Otto, the gray squirrel, who
came to tell Jeremiah that he had changed
his mind about moving. "It seems to me that
you have a very strong position here," he
said to Tapiola; "the ground is all in your
favor." "I am glad you think so," replied

Tapiola, with satisfaction, "but I am surprised to see you here, for I was led to believe that you had already started for the West." "What I heard about the West did not please me," said Otto, "so I thought I would stay here, and dig a little hole." "That is all very well," said Jeremiah, "but I have a contract to move your belongings to New Jersey." "I think I will keep them in my own little hole," said Otto. "They will be safer there." "He that diggeth a pit shall fall into it," said Jeremiah; "and whoso breaketh through a wall, a serpent shall bite him."

This conversation was interrupted by the sudden arrival of Peabody, who had decided not to wait for the outcome of the war, before doing business. "How does it happen," he asked indignantly, "that my concern was not

allowed to bid on the supplies for your regiment?" Tapiola replied that the Quartermaster General had charge of all contracts.
"Then let me see him at once," cried Peabody, "for too much time has been wasted."

"What," asked Jeremiah in business-like
tones, "do you wish to see me about?"
"Come, come," said Peabody testily, "do not
take that tone with me. I am the head of a
large concern, and I am full of enthusiasm."
"Very well, then," said Jeremiah more politely; "what can I do for you?" "That is
better," said Peabody, "but it is not the question. The question is, what can we do for each
other." "Do you wish to sell me supplies?"
asked Jeremiah. "I must tell you that I already have all that I need, including a half
dozen of the finest assorted buttons, which

I do not know what to do with." "Are they large, or small?" asked Peabody. "On the whole, small," said Jeremiah, "and very fine; though one of them is large, and of great beauty." "Let us talk it over," said Peabody.

Half an hour later, Peabody was observed leaving the camp, with a dazzled expression, and with a bag of buttons. "What have you there?" asked Tapiola curiously, "and did your business with the Quartermaster General turn out to your liking?" "I cannot say," replied Peabody; "but I have bought a bag of buttons." "Well, well," said Tapiola, "I did not know that you were in the button business." "I am only in it a quarter of an hour," said Peabody unhappily.

When the first lamps of evening were

lighted in the city, Matilda came to see
Henry. "Henry," she breathed, emerging
like a gray shadow from the twilight air. "Is
it you, Matilda?" asked Henry, "or am I
dreaming?" "What a way to greet your
wife," said Matilda, with a smile. "I can as-
sure you that I am all too solid flesh." And
with a sigh, she added, "I am afraid that my
figure is not what it used to be." "It is the
figure of an angel, in any case," said Henry
fervently.

"I have missed you," said Matilda gravely.
"It is disconcerting to come around a corner,
and not to find you waiting. One hardly
knows what to do." "I have missed you, too,"
said Henry; "in the long watches of the
night, I have thought of you, Matilda; and
then, sometimes in the darkness, it has

seemed to me as though I saw you plain."
"Indeed," said Matilda nervously. "And
what was I doing?" "You were sleeping,"
said Henry tenderly, "with your head under
your wing." "Was I indeed?" said Matilda,
with a gratified expression. "I am so glad
that you saw me.

"As a matter of fact," she continued, after
a moment, "I do not find the life of a grass
widow at all agreeable. Everyone wishes to
take advantage of me. . . . To be a lone
female is to be the victim of every kind of
accident. And then, besides," she added
breathlessly, "there are the starlings."

She continued: "I did not mind when your
friend took me home; but since then he has
brought at least a dozen of his friends along
with him. They are not very amusing, to tell

the truth; they talk all the time, but only
about the starving masses." "That is not
very entertaining," agreed Henry with re-
lief, "but at least they are serious-minded."
"I do not think that is anything in their
favor," said Matilda. "And there is something else, besides."

Coming closer to Henry, she looked fear-
fully around, and dropped her voice. "From
what my friend tells me," she said in low
tones, "I believe that they aim to take over
the entire Cathedral, the north and south
buttresses, and all four spires." "They are
mad," said Henry simply; "the pigeons will
never allow it." "Perhaps not," said Matilda
doubtfully, "but the starlings are great
talkers." "As for the south buttress," said
Henry stoutly, "nothing would surprise me;

but they will never take the north." "Just the same," said Matilda, "they have won over several of the younger pigeons to their ideas."

"When the war is over," said Henry, "I will deal with the starlings, and with all the other inconveniences." "The truth is," said Matilda, "they do not expect you to return at all, except in a mutilated condition." "It is too bad," said Henry swallowing, "that people cannot mind their own business in this world."

Presently he burst out, in muffled tones: "What a flood of anguish is poured upon the earth. The dark is all around us; our little ark rocks upon the waters. Oh weak and sinful generation, the dove shall seek a sign in vain, for all is waste and evil here.

"I trust that you are well, Matilda," he added politely.

"I am well enough," said Matilda, "what with worry, and lack of sleep. I must admit that this constant talk of your remains has begun to unsettle me." "Have courage," said Henry bravely; "I am not remains yet."

"Do you wear the little feather boa I gave you?" she asked. "Yes indeed," said Henry; "it is very comfortable." "Do not wear it if it rains," she said, "for the feathers will get wet." "If it rains," said Henry, "I will put it in a dry place." "You know, I should not like to have anything happen to you," she said. "We have been together a long time, and one grows used to things." "I hope it has not seemed too long to you," said Henry humbly; "it has not seemed so long to me."

"That is very sweet," said Maltilda. "I did not really mean that it had been too long . . . but perhaps because I am young, the time does not go so fast." "That is true," said Henry soberly; "to me, the days seem to end almost before they have begun." "Poor Henry," said Matilda gently, "you should have married someone your own age." "I know," said Henry, "but I did not care for them."

For a while they sat together in the deepening twilight, without speaking—two small and lonely souls in the vast wilderness of the night. Poor Matilda, thought Henry, I have not been a very good husband for her. And Matilda thought: poor Henry, he has not had much happiness in life. "Will you be all right, Matilda," asked Henry at length, "until the war is over, and I am able to come home again?" "Do not worry about me," she said; "I shall manage." "When peace comes," said Henry, "we will take a little vacation in the south." "That will be nice," said Matilda; "I have always wanted to do

that." "They say the mocking bird is very fine," said Henry.

"Is there any little comfort you would like?" asked Matilda, rising to go. "I could use a few soft pieces of paper," said Henry, "to make myself more easy in my tree." "I will see that you get them," said Matilda. "And a little piece of bread," said Henry, "preferably crust, because I find that a steady diet of cheese does not agree with me."

"I must go now," said Matilda. "Good-bye, dear Henry; I will let you know about the starlings." "Please do," said Henry; "and do not worry about me, I will be home before you know it." "If I am not there," said Matilda, "I will leave a note for you; but in that case I shall probably be at my

mother's." "Good-bye, Matilda," said
Henry, "and God bless you."

And he climbed again into his tree, to
watch the southern sky until Richard appeared to relieve him.

Below him, in the deep shadow of a bench,
Jeremiah and his grandson were talking.
"Have you written home recently?" asked
Jeremiah. "I should not like your mother to
be uneasy on your account." Micah replied
that he had written to his mother that morning. "And did you tell her about me?" asked
Jeremiah, trying to appear indifferent.
"Naturally," said Micah, "for I was burst-
ing with pride." "I doubt if she will appre-
ciate what I did," said Jeremiah, "but there
is no harm in mentioning it." "I do not see
any harm either," said Micah, "particularly

as we have not had very much to boast about in our family." "You are mistaken," said Jeremiah, "but all that is beside the point."

He continued: "Do not imagine that your family is without distinction, Micah. Some of your ancestors were companions to the saints, and shared their holy lives; while others devoted themselves to science, and perished bravely in the laboratories of Pasteur, Carrel, and Dr. Alfred Meyer. However, it is to the future that we must look, rather than to the past. The cycle of success is three generations, from shirt-sleeves to shirt-sleeves. Today we are poor; but tomorrow we may be rich, provided that you seize every opportunity to improve yourself." "I have no other wish," said Micah humbly, "than to improve myself; and I

hope to be made a Corporal very soon."
"There is no future in the army," said Jeremiah, with a sigh; "not even in the quartermaster corps; you will notice that the best
Generals retire as soon as possible, and
become the heads of large corporations."
"Then what am I doing in the army?" asked
Micah unhappily. "You are helping your
old grandfather," said Jeremiah.

He continued: "What I have in mind for
you, Micah, is a small business, preferably in
the clothing field, or in insurance; after
which, if you are successful, there is nothing
to keep you from going into the theater, or
even into the films." "I am sure that you
know best, Grandfather," said Micah, "and
I will try very hard; but just the same, I
would like to be a Corporal."

The night deepened around them; the stars shone in the sky; and in the tree above them, Henry, rousing from slumber, lifted his head from his wing, and cried in muffled tones, "All's well."

''SOFIA IS TAKEN,''
said the newspapers next day; and Richard,
returning from a routine flight, declared,
"We have suffered a serious defeat."

This news saddened the little terrier, who
believed that the war was lasting a long time.
But he would not allow himself to become

discouraged, and remarked, "It is possible
that she was taken by surprise." And de-
termined to find out how things were for
himself, he exclaimed, "Richard, let us go
forth together, and carry out a raid upon the
enemy lines." This suggestion was opposed
by Richard with all his might. "We are doing very well here," he said; "we are holding
our own; I do not see anything to be gained
by such an excursion." "In a war of movement," replied Tapiola, "it is sometimes sensible to sit back, and let the other fellow wear
himself out; but in a war of nerves, it is ex-
pedient to give an occasional hop." "That
may be so," said Richard grudgingly, "but
why me? Why do you not take Micah or
Henry with you?" "Richard," said Tapiola
earnestly, "we have been friends of long

standing, and we have shared many dangers
and discomforts together. Do you think, if I
fall, that I should like to expire in the arms
of Micah, who is an ordinary private, and
without experience?" "I do not see what that
has to do with it," said Richard; "two minutes later, it will not make the least difference to you in whose arms you have expired."

He continued in a gloomy vein: "Only
the artist can take a practical view of things,
because he does not draw unnecessary dis-
tinctions. He understands that in order to
succeed, he must make a certain effect; and
that the details are not important, as long as
they assist in this effect. I shall be happy to
pipe The Soldier's Lament over you, if you
perish; but it will be on practical, rather
than esthetic grounds, to arouse our side to

sterner and nobler feelings. How you perish
is of no interest to me; I will make it sound
grand, in any event, but you will not be there
to notice." "What has come over you, my
friend?" cried Tapiola. "I do not recognize
you; is this the singer whose whole life has
been devoted to the worship of beauty?" "It
is a mistake to worship beauty," said Richard
somberly, "for there is no beauty in death,
and death is all one will find at the end."
"You are mistaken," said Tapiola; "the last
words of the poet often ennoble those who
come after." "The last words of Shelley,"
said Richard, "were a mumble, lost in the
waters of the Mediterranean; and Byron's
last poem ended with the lines, 'The worm,
the canker, and the grief, Are mine alone.'
Correct me if I am wrong." "You are right,"

said Tapiola, abashed at this display of learning, "or at least very nearly; but some-one has told you, for you did not know all that by yourself." "I have been talking to Henry," Richard admitted, "and I have decided that art without religion is not the comfort it is supposed to be. Hereafter I intend to apply myself to the works of Palestrina, Sankey, and Mr. Samuel Webbe." "Very well," said Tapiola, "but first let us have a look at the tigers."

"In my opinion," remarked Tapiola, as he crawled on his belly along the path to the Zoo, with Richard fluttering in the rear, "too much is made of the question of utility in art. To what does art address itself? To the soul. But how is it possible to be useful to the soul? We do not even know where it is located." "It is in the back, between the wings," said Richard, "and it leaves the body by means of an upward spiral." "I believe that it is seated in the nose," said Tapiola, "for that is where the sweetest odors are to be found. Therefore art should be fragrant, and have a lasting quality." "On the contrary," said Richard, "art should be melodious; it should soar into the sky on wings of song." "To me," said Tapiola, "the artist will speak of homely things, in such a way as to make them appear more aromatic." "An artist," said Richard, "should also speak of the mysteries; he should be at home in the loftiest realms of the spirit."

But he agreed that art itself ought not to be mysterious. "The trouble today," he said, "is that our musicians no longer appeal to the ear; and our poets no longer speak to the mind. It is in music today that one must look for meaning without sound; and in poetry that one finds sound without meaning. I believe that there is something fishy here." "Try to move a little faster," said Tapiola impatiently; "you are holding up the progress of the patrol."

"All we need now," said Richard, "is painters who do not know how to draw, and then we will be thoroughly in the soup." "I believe that we are already in enemy territory," observed Tapiola, sniffing the air, "for I can smell tigers; and there is another odor, which I imagine to be an aurochs." "Then let us go home," said Richard promptly, "before they find us; for we have already been braver than necessary." "I have never smelled an aurochs before," said Tapiola; "yet the odor is familiar, and not unpleasant." "What does it smell like?" asked Richard. "Like popcorn," said Tapiola.

At this moment, Nuba, the lion, waking from a nap, let out a thunderous roar, which echoed among the walks and paths, and filled the Park in that vicinity with sound. He was answered by the oldest seal, from his pool; and by the little Indian elephant in her cage in another corner of the Zoo. In the aviary, the parrots began to scream; and the gibbons, swinging from their bars in the monkey house, chattered and cried. "We are surrounded," exclaimed Tapiola; and tucking his tail firmly between his legs, he fled back to camp, belly to the ground, and upon the heels of the wind. When he arrived, pale and out of breath, Richard was already hiding under the supply wagon. "We have had a narrow escape," said Tapiola; "I would not be surprised if we had stumbled upon the main body of the foe." "No matter," said Richard, whose bill was still chattering, "we are home now; but I believe that there is something to be said for a negotiated peace, after all." "Never," exclaimed Tapiola; "I shall fight to the end; but I do not think I shall attack again, at least until morning."

Micah, who had been awakened by the precipitate return of the two officers, now stepped forward, and saluting his commander, remarked: "All is quiet, Sir; the starlings are asleep on the roof of the Museum." "What is that to us?" cried Richard indignantly. "We have been in danger." "I thought you would like to know," said Micah simply. And he added modestly, "After all, that is all I have to report."

"You have done well," said Tapiola. "I do not think that there will be any further alarms. Goodnight, Micah; you may go to sleep now, if you wish." "If you do not mind," said Micah, "I will stay awake, and think about the clothing business." "What is there to think about, in the clothing business?" asked Richard.

"I am young," said Micah, "and wherever I start, I must start at the bottom. But even the bottom is a serious thing; and if I am to improve myself, the sooner I begin to think about it, the better." "There is no improvement in sight for business," said Richard; "the war has seen to that." "I intend to seek my real future in the theater," said Micah.

This remark, so unexpected, caused Richard to start, and to glance hastily at the young rat, whose simple and earnest expression did not change. "The theater?" he exclaimed; "are you an actor?" "I do not have to be an actor," replied Micah, "to produce a play." "You do not know anything about the theater," cried Richard indignantly. "That is true," said Micah, "but I shall know a great deal about the clothing business."

He continued: "I must tell you, this is not all my own idea, but my grandfather's. His nose tells him what is good or bad, and he believes that this is the best thing for me." "And have you ever seen a play?" asked Richard, "or an opera?" "No," said Micah, "but I do not think that makes any difference."

"I am an old hand at this," said Richard; "I know a great deal about the stage, from having been a singer." "Then perhaps you will help me," said Micah humbly, "for I am sure that I have a lot to learn." "The best thing to start with," said Richard, "is an operetta; it is expensive to produce, but the rewards are great." "What is an operetta?" asked Micah. "Let me give you an example," said Richard; and filling his lungs, and puffing out his chest, he first tried one or two notes in several registers, after which he burst out with the Street Song from Naughty Marietta.

When he had finished, his face fell, and he remarked gloomily, "However, I am all through with that sort of thing." At this, Micah took a step backward in surprise. "Are you in earnest?" he exclaimed. "Do you really intend to give up your career, when everything is so favorable?" "For some time," said Richard with a gentle smile, "I have been inclined toward the spiritual life. I intend to retire, and to seek happiness in some modest retreat, within sound of the Cathedral bells." "It is a pity," said Micah regretfully, "for I have never heard a voice like yours, so high, so loud, and so gymnastic." "It is a fact," Richard admitted, "that the voice is a good one, though I dare say it could be improved." And he gave a light laugh. "I do not see how it could be improved," said Micah, "for it seems to me already at the peak of excellence." "Do you think so?" asked Richard with a satisfied air.

"Of course," he remarked after a moment, "if I were to receive a really tempting offer . . . It would have to be rather a large offer," he added hastily, smoothing the feathers of his breast, "for I am really looking forward to retiring from the stage." "Well," said Micah simply, "first of all I have to go through the clothing business; but afterwards I will come and talk to you about an operetta." "Do," said Richard; "who knows, perhaps I will be ready to come out of my retirement by then."

With these words, he went off to look for the quilt, and finding Tapiola already beneath it, got in beside him, at the same time managing to give the little terrier several

~~~~~~

sharp pecks with his beak, to make him move over.

Micah retired to his position beneath the wagon; Henry drowsed upon his branch; and Jeremiah, on the hill by the obelisk, curled himself up in the grass, to sleep. "Behold," he murmured, closing his eyes, "waters rise up out of the north. They have chased me sore like a bird, they that are mine enemies without cause. Baldness is come upon Gaza; Ashkelon is brought to nought. Make sharp the arrows, and hold firm the shields; our pursuers are upon our necks. O thou sword of Jehovah, how long will it be ere thou be quiet? Put thyself into thy scabbard; rest, and be still."

He sighed a little to himself. "A leopard shall watch against their cities," he said drowsily. His voice grew fainter and fainter; he slept, and all the camp was quiet.

Far off, to the south, beneath the spires of the Cathedral, Matilda watched from her cornice. Her expression was grave and tender, and she paid no attention to the starling at her side. Her thoughts were on Henry, and she murmured, as though she were speaking to him, "Is it possible that I have misjudged you? Can it be that I have not known until now the true state of my feelings?" And turning to the starling, she exclaimed, "Why do you not go back to the Museum where you belong?"

"Because it does not suit me," replied the starling simply; "it is more comfortable here. What has happened?" "You would not understand," said Matilda; "but I can tell you this: that I have had a glimpse into the devoted heart of one individual." "There is no such thing as one individual," said the starling; "there is only the party. I have told you that the days of the private individual are over." "We are still free," said Matilda, "to fly aloft upon our errands in the sky. We are still free to speak, in the darkness of night, to that great spirit, beneath whose downy breast and ever-sheltering wings we seek our little crumbs of bread. We are still free to comfort the oppressed; we are still free to love." "There is no such word as 'free,'" said the starling; and he added calmly, "those little weaknesses you mention will be taken care of by the committee." "Leave me," said Matilda, with a cry; "I wish to be alone." And she gave him a sharp buffet with her wings. Losing his balance, the starling clawed desperately at the stone, to keep from falling. "What are you doing?" he exclaimed; "this is a free country; you have no right to bite me. Where are the police?"

MR. EDWARD HERRING-
way, an assistant keeper at the Zoo, stepped
out of the honeybear's cage, carrying a pail
of water in his hand. As he turned to fasten
the gate, his attention was drawn to a com-
motion among the seals; he stepped forward, to peer in that direction, leaving the

cage closed, but not locked. Thereafter, he forgot about it, and continued on toward the grizzlies.

The honeybear, a brown friendly little fellow, came to the door of his cage to watch Mr. Herringway go off. The door rattled a little, and he gave it an enquiring tap with his long claws. It seemed to be loose . . .

Ten minutes later, the cage was empty, and the honeybear was hiding in the shadows of the Sixty-Fifth Street tunnel, thinking things over.

He had no burning desire for freedom, but he had a great deal of curiosity. He did not wish to bother anybody; fortunately, there did not seem to be anyone about. The path went north, through shadows and un-der lamplight; there were trees on either

side, and grassy hills; and it disappeared in
the misty distance. It looked interesting, and
he decided to follow it.

From Sixty-fifth to Seventy-second
Street, his progress was slow, but joyful,
and without incident. He climbed a tree, but

there was nothing there, and he came down again. He examined a little summer house made of wood; it was empty, and smelled of children; he broke off a bit of flowering bush, and tried the taste.

At Seventy-second Street he crossed the drive, and started down the hill. It was here, and at this moment, that Amy saw him, his silhouette looming above her as she stood beside the lake, where she had gone to carry home some water to her mother. For a second, while her heart stopped beating, she stared in horror at the ominous bulk between her and the sky; then, with a gasp, she turned, and tore for the Museum.

Micah heard her squeaks while she was still some distance away, and ran forward to help her. Breathless and trembling, she threw herself upon his bosom. "It has come," she announced in a tragic voice; "the war is here. The enemy is behind me, laying waste the world." "I had better sound the alarm," said Micah, "for I imagine that the battle is about to begin."

And he went to report the news to his Colonel.

Tapiola received the message in silence, and with a calm mien. He ordered the regiment paraded; and when they were drawn up in line, he appeared before them with a serious air, and addressed them as follows:

"Officers and men of the Twenty Seventh . . . the moment for which we have been waiting has arrived. The enemy has crossed the drive in force, and his advance units have reached the west shore of the lake. This attack comes in the dark hours of the night, and at a time when I was not expecting it, but it does not find me unprepared. I have studied the map; and I think I can say that I have made the best possible disposition of the forces at my command. You, Henry, will go aloft, to bomb the foe at the Seventy-Eighth Street underpass, and Micah will go with you, to oppose him on the ground. Richard will inspire us from a tree; and Jeremiah will mind the spike. I myself shall observe the battle from the base of the obelisk. The order of the day is Victory; but that does not mean that the war is over. Go now to your positions, my friends, and prepare to do battle for the honor of the regiment.

"There will be bandages and refreshments in the rear."

So saying, and with a grave and martial bearing, he turned away. "I do not feel very much like singing," said Richard; "my stomach is upset from so much worry." "In that case," said Tapiola, "you may come with me to the obelisk, and carry messages to the forward units of the command." "I do not think that I can fly," said Richard; "my bowels are so loose." "Richard," exclaimed Tapiola, losing his temper, "I do not care what you do, but please do not bother me about your bowels." "At least I am honest," said Richard, "and do not pretend to be braver than I feel."

Standing before the spike, erect and sober, Jeremiah bade farewell to his grandson. "Good-bye, Micah," he said; "I do not know what you will find where you are going, but if it is large, try to get behind it. For in the dark, it is sometimes possible to surprise a foe, and defeat him from a safe distance. Do not be afraid to use your wits, as in the case of the Midianites and the Amalekites, whom Gideon smote in the valley of Jezreel. He had but three hundred, against a host; but he divided them, and gave them trumpets and pitchers, with which to make a great sound. The Midianites and Amalekites were surprised at this maneuver; and the host fled as far as Bethshittah, in considerable confusion." "Alas," said Micah, "I am only one and not three hundred, and I have neither trumpet nor pitcher." "I should have provided them," said Jeremiah with a sigh. "I do not suppose that you have a sling shot, and a smooth pebble?" "I have nothing but

my teeth," said Micah, "and a stout heart."
"Well," said Jeremiah, whose own teeth
were yellow and dull with age, "that is all
your ancestors had."

But as his grandson turned to go, he drew
him close once more, and embraced him. "I
do not know if I did right to let you join this
war, my child," he said, "and if anything
happens to you, I shall regret it." "Do not
be afraid, Grandfather," said Micah bravely,
"for God will protect me." "He hath estab-
lished the world by His wisdom," said Jeremiah gravely, "and perhaps He will."

With these words, he returned to his spike,
and Micah marched away toward the south,
with Henry circling protectively above him.

At the underpass they halted, while
Henry flew up onto the parapet, to recon-

noiter. Presently he flew down again; and Micah whispered, "Did you see anything?" "Yes," said Henry, speaking low; "the enemy is approaching." "What does he look like?" asked Micah eagerly. "He is a horrid looking object," said Henry.

"I am a little nervous," he admitted, as he sharpened his beak upon a stone.

Finding a slight depression in which to hide, Micah set himself to wait. His heart was beating strongly, and his mouth was dry, but he was not afraid. It seemed to him that the climax of his life was at hand, and that before the morning broke, everything would be changed for him. He saw himself returning home after the battle, a Corporal and a hero; and he imagined the serious talks that he would have with Amy when the war was over. His mother's face appeared before him in the darkness, and he smiled at her. "You will have no reason to be ashamed of me," he said. At the same time, he felt a lump in his throat, and his eyes grew moist, against his will.

The night hung clear and still above the earth, the lamps of the Park making a misty glow here and there in the darkness. All was silent; beyond, in the city, something hooted, dim and far away. "Can you see anything?" asked Micah, shivering a little in the cold night air. "I think he is coming nearer," said Henry.

A moment later he remarked in a firm voice, "It is time." And with a single cry, "Matilda," he rose upon his wings, and launched himself at the honeybear, who, taken by surprise, fell over onto his back. At the same time, Micah scrambled from his trench, and charging across the intervening ground, closed his eyes, and gave the honey-bear a sharp nip on the leg.

On the hill by the obelisk, Tapiola and Richard were waiting for news of the battle. "I do not hear anything," said Tapiola. "Our troops are not yet engaged." And as he strained to see through the darkness, he thought: Only a few days ago, I was leading a literary life at Mrs. Poppel's. Now I am here, on a hill in the night, fighting for freedom. But perhaps there is not as much difference as I thought; for whether one is on a hill, or under a sofa, the important thing is, what is one doing there? Battles and books have changed the course of history before this, the one as much as the other. Perhaps it would have been wiser for me to stay at home, to help Mrs. Poppel. But the truth is, that to the poet, a single blow is more satisfying than a poem. And so, I was carried away . . . I am not sure that I was right. For who now will play with my ball, and my little bone made of rubber, amusing the guests, and creating an atmosphere of joy? Those things also are necessary to civilization. My little basket will stand empty in its corner, a mute reminder of my heroism, and my fate; but in the years to come, my absence will be felt in the publishing business. There is another courage, besides that of the soldier; it is to stay at home, doing the work at hand, without glory and without acclaim.

Dear Mrs. P., if I do not return, believe that I have laid down my life to enable you to publish the works of Mr. Nathan, Mme. Undset, and Thomas Mann.

Turning to Richard, he exclaimed: "See that my remains are wrapped in my eiderdown quilt, for death is a cold and lonely land, and I shall want to take with me all the warmth and friendliness my heart can carry." "Very well," said Richard unhappily, "but it seems a great pity, for there is only the one quilt, and winter is coming." "You will be home before winter," said Tapiola; "the war is almost over." "I am glad to hear it," said Richard, "for I am considering an offer in the theater."

"I thought that you intended to retire," said Tapiola in surprise, "and lead a spiritual life." "That is true," said Richard, "and I have not changed my mind; but I think that it is possible to lead a more spiritual life after having been a great success."

At this moment, the sound of fighting was wafted to them from the underpass, where the attack had begun. "Hark," said Tapiola; "the battle is joined. Our advance forces are in action." "That sounds like Micah to me," said Richard, as a shrill squeal split the air; "he is in trouble." "Then we had better go at once to his assistance," said Tapiola. "Let us wait for another squeal," said Richard.

A second cry, louder, and full of anguish, rose through the darkness from the underpass. "Come," said Tapiola; "we dare delay no longer, or the battle will be lost." And taking a deep breath, he cried,

"Forward, the Twenty Seventh."

And with the added cry of "Victory and Mrs. Poppel," he dashed slowly down the hill.

"I will go and see what Jeremiah is doing," said Richard.

The canary found the Quartermaster

General pacing nervously up and down in front of his spike. "How goes the battle?" he asked, as soon as he caught sight of Richard; "I have heard some very distressing sounds." "All is lost," replied Richard despondently; "I fear that your grandson has perished." "And Tapiola?" demanded Jeremiah loudly; "where is he, and where are the reserves?" "He has gone to see for himself," said Richard. "As for the reserves, I believe that they are us." "Then what are we waiting for?" cried Jeremiah; "let us attack at once, and save what we can." "Very well," said Richard gloomily, "if you think so; but if we lose the reserves, we shall have nothing left at all." "Are you afraid?" cried Jeremiah. "Yes," said Richard. "Then I implore you to be brave," said Jeremiah. "Honesty like mine also takes courage," said Richard.

"It is too late to debate the point," said Jeremiah, with a groan; "let us go." He had no sooner spoken, than Amy ran up to them, her face bright with resolve. "Let me go with you," she cried, "to help, in my poor way." "Are you not frightened?" asked Jeremiah tenderly. "No," she said proudly, "for my heart is bigger than my fears."

And she added: "It is the women who must bind up the wounds of this war."

Taking the bandages, she followed Jeremiah, who led the way with the spike, while Richard flew up into a tree, to act as observer.

As Jeremiah had feared, they were too late; when they arrived at the underpass, the battle was already over. Weary of the conflict, which he had not expected, and did not enjoy, the honeybear had retired, nursing his paw where Micah had bitten it. Seated upon the battlefield, which now was theirs, the victors attempted to get their breath, Tapiola upon his haunches with his tongue hanging out, and Henry amidst a fluff of loose feathers in the grass. But Micah lay upon his side with his eyes closed, and the life blood draining from two great wounds in his belly.

They gathered about him in silence, while Amy attempted to stanch the blood, and Jeremiah strove to master his grief. Richard was the first to speak; with an expression of anguish, he remarked, "This is the end of my hopes; my career in the theater is finished." And seeking out Henry, he said to him with a dejected air, "Now I have learned the futility of worldly ambitions."

Amy had Micah's weary head pillowed on her lap. "Micah," she said, "can you hear me? It is I, Amy, your friend. I am here to hold you. The battle is over, and you have won a great victory. I am so proud of you . . . But do not try to move. Rest, now; the war is ended." "Amy," said Micah, opening his eyes, "is it you? Do not go away." And he added simply, "I did the best I could."

Turning his head, he saw Jeremiah in the crowd around him. "You, too, Grandfather?" he said wonderingly. "God did His best for me."

But a spasm of pain shook him, and he cried,

"It hurts."

Jeremiah knelt beside him, smiling, while the tears ran down his cheeks. "Micah, my little one," he said gently, "you must try to bear it bravely. It will not hurt for long."

Micah's eyes searched his grandfather's face. "Am I dying, Grandfather?" he asked at length; and Jeremiah inclined his head. The young soldier took a deep breath. "Talk to me, then," he whispered.

"Micah," said Jeremiah, "you are going into a cool and lovely land. There the sweet colors of the evening live, the deep blue sky of night. Where you are going, it is wide and clear and beautiful and free; there is no sadness there, and no regret. The stars will shine around you, making a peaceful glory; and you will hear the friendly winds forever speaking with quiet voices. You will be happy there, Micah, my son."

"Will it not be lonely, Grandfather?" asked Micah.

"No," said Jeremiah; "for love goes with you, and will never leave you. It is in your heart, Micah, my son. And we who stay behind you here, will join you in a little while . . . in a little while."

"Yes, Grandfather," said Micah, smiling. And he added, with a sigh,

"I wish I were a Corporal."

Deeply moved, Tapiola stepped forward, and in a low voice remarked, "Then receive your promotion now, upon this very field your bravery has won for us." So saying, he embraced Micah, and declared, "From now on, you are a Corporal."

Micah beckoned Jeremiah to bend closer. "Tell Mother," he whispered; "she will be so proud." His eyes, which shone with pain and with surprise, grew dim. "See, it is morning," he said; "the night is over." And later,

"It is the peaceful day."

They were his last words. Tapiola covered him with the quilt, and ordered the silk banner of the regiment to be laid across it. On a low branch above the bier, Richard sang a last farewell; and Henry read from the Psalms:

The Lord is my Shepherd; I shall not want.

He maketh me to lie down in green pastures.

He leadeth me beside still waters.

Jeremiah stood above his grandson, with bent head. "Farewell, Micah, my son," he said. "Now you are free, of pain and sadness; and no loss can touch you. It is for us to weep, who still are captive here; who see the sun by day and the moon by night, and strive to comfort our hearts with small changes. But for you there is the wide and endless sky, and the peace that passeth understanding." And as he mourned, he repeated to himself the words, "Turn again our captivity, O Lord, as the streams in the South."

Slowly and sadly, Tapiola turned away. "The war is over," he said. "It is time to go home."

And as he passed beneath the tree on which Richard was sitting, he added under his breath,

"We have lost the flower of our youth."

On his branch, Richard looked down at him with an exasperated expression. "What else did you expect?" he asked.

T H E days went by, the tulips
bloomed along the walks, and the grass grew
green on Micah's grave. And Tapiola, with
a new ribbon in his hair, walked in the Park
with Mrs. Poppel's maid, Margot, and said
to his friend Otto, the squirrel,

"The war is over; and the aurochs have retired into the mists of history. It is a new world, fresh with spring, in which everyone can be happy and free. What is your opinion?"

To this, Otto replied: "I confess, I have not seen any of the fruits of victory. The costs of the war were such that I have been unable to put anything by; and in addition, I am still waiting to get my furniture back from New Jersey." "How is that?" asked Tapiola in surprise; "when I last saw you, you had decided to keep it here." "That is true," said Otto, "but Jeremiah would not hear of it. He said that now that he had a wagon, it was too bad not to use it." "And could you think of nothing to say to that?" asked Tapiola, laughing. "What could I say?" replied Otto unhappily; "he is a veteran. And besides, it seems that we had a contract."

"I am a veteran too," said the starling, "but my battles have been fought against poverty and injustice. No one respects me on that account, and I have had to move from the Cathedral back to the Museum again. I do not for a minute admit that you have any right to these savings of yours, but I would rather have them here, where I can keep my eye on them, than in New Jersey. Tell Jeremiah to bring them back again." "Unfortunately," said Otto, "he has sold his wagon to a Mr. Peabody, and is no longer in the moving business." "What business is he in?" asked Tapiola curiously. "The button business," said Otto sadly.

Tapiola returned home, and retired under

the sofa. There he lay, with his head on his
paws, and considered the world, which he
could see had not been helped by his efforts.
Is it possible, he thought, that our sacrifices

were in vain? And yet, he decided, even
though I have not been able to change anybody's mind, I could not have done other-
wise. For if freedom is a thistle, full of pains,
it is never-the-less a lovely flower, and the
fields would be bare and dismal without it.
Had the aurochs succeeded, there would be
nothing but cabbages in the world. We must

fight for the thistle, but we must not cry out when it stings us.

And seeing again the little household bug, he said to him, "You did not know Mrs. Poppel, and yet it is her house in which you live." "It is a very poor one, then," said the bug; "I can think of several improvements I would like to make." "My friend," said Tapiola sadly, "when you have made them, you will find another bug who objects to them."

And in a thoughtful mood, he curled up in his basket, under the new quilt that Mrs. Poppel had bought for him.

This book is composed in Linotype "Scotch."
This style of type came into fashion in England
and the United States by way of fonts cast at
the foundry of Alex. Wilson & Son at Glasgow
in 1833. It was a style of letter that echoed the
"classical" taste of the time, and would seem to
have been inspired by the kind of letter-shapes
that result when you cut lettering on a copper
plate with a graver—just as visiting-cards are
cut now. It is more precise and *vertical* in char-
acter than the "old style" types (such as Cas-
lon) that it displaced.

———————

*This book was composed, printed and bound
by* H. WOLFF, *New York.*

Tapiola's Brave Regiment

IN THESE DAYS of darkness, with wars abroad and mistrust at home, every hero must be prepared to do his part. So at least thought Tapiola, the Yorkshire terrier with the shaggy coat and the ribbon in his hair who lived with Mrs. Poppel of the publishing family, and in a manner of speaking took care of her. Now Tapiola was not one to be content with fine-spun theorizing and complacent comfort. For him the deed geared to the thought, the strong idea made stronger by action.

Thus it was that, when he came to believe the country stood in need of brave hearts and stout hands, Tapiola immediately sprang to the defense of all that which he held dear. The enemy, the dreaded aurochs resurgent from a forgotten time, was at the gates. (No one had seen him, the press carried no word of the matter; but Tapiola *knew* he was on the march.) The authorities, unbelievably blind to the menace, did nothing whatever. Not so our hero. With his old friends Richard the canary and Jeremiah the rat, he planned and perfected a military organization to meet the foe on the field of battle.

This is the story of their amazing campaign, their privations and endurances, their difficulties with supply-lines, profiteers, camp-followers, and an indifferent civilian population. How they won through despite all obstacles, how they met the invader and put him to flight, make as delicious a small gem as Robert Nathan has ever written.